IF BLACK HAD CLAIMED HIS QUEEN

Angelia Vernon Menchan 2021

Honorable MENCHAN Media LLC

An Alternate Reality Story

We have all wondered what would occur if one simple thing occurred. In my book, Black's Obsession, Malcolm Black bungles so many opportunities to tell Cinnamon Dubois his true feelings. He pretended they were cool, just friends for years. In fact, everyone seems to know his feelings but her.

Malcolm returns after graduate school to tell her... and discovers Cinnamon is with another man because he's waited four years. He leaves enraged and never returns until she's about to be married. He spends decades wondering what would have occurred with one minor change. In IF BLACK HAD CLAIMED HIS QUEEN: An Alternate Reality story we get to see exactly what would have occurred had he opened his mouth and spoke his love...

The summer Malcolm Black graduated with an MBA he packed up his car to drive home to Center City. The girl of his dreams, Cinnamon Dubois had graduated high school and two years of college and he was finally going to reveal his feelings. Malcolm fell hard for her when she was a ninth grader, but she was too young and pure for him...then. They were best friends and stayed in touch, but he never revealed his true feelings to her. He watched her date boys he felt unworthy of her, at the time he felt unworthy. He certainly had his share of sexual escapades but felt he waited for her... to be old enough and ready for his real feelings.

Many *people told me to stay away but this year I'm going for it*. Malcolm thought as he sped along interstate ten... home.

CHAPTER ONE

1974

MALCOLM

Once home Malcolm rested, he spent time with his mom, telling her his plans. Two years earlier she told him to stay away from Cinnamon; she was too young and innocent.

"I'm telling Cinnamon I'm in love with her mom." Amelia Black was a stoic, no nonsense type peering at him over the rim of her glasses.

"I sure do hope you got the entire g-spot player shit out your system and you don't stand in the way of her education. You've been experiencing life for years, but she's not had that chance."

"Mom, I know that but I'm going to date her, throw my hat in the ring. My insecurities and your advice stopped me from telling her years ago but I'm not waiting for the next man to snap her up." She nodded and went back to her breakfast preparations. His mind was made up.

~~ɏɏɏɏɏ~~

The next day Malcolm drove out to where she lived, when he got there, she was sitting on the porch reading and drinking lemonade. He thought she looked so beautiful. She was wearing a wild colored short dress and her hair piled on top of her head in a bushy ponytail, and looked kissed by the sun, she looked just like her name. He got up and walked up to the porch where she sat on an old wooden swing. Seeing him she smiled brightly, her eyes twinkling.

"Hey beautiful, how've you been?"

"Lovely, just lovely, I'm glad to be done with high school and two years of college through dual enrollment. I'm now a grown ass woman."

"What are you going to do about more school?"

"I'm going to the University of Florida next year." Malcolm was surprised because he knew how her mom felt about Black schools and thought at a minimum, she would attend her mom's alma mater, Bethune Cookman in Daytona.

After idle conversation, she stared at him, posing a startling question.

"Do you please all of those women that you have sex with. I hope you are ensuring all of those girls have orgasms, because if not you're a sorry brother." Hearing her say that gave him an erection. He moved a bit to hide it.

"Of course, I do, I'm all about pleasing a woman, why go there if not for that reason."

"I have taken my first lover, and he sure does know how to please a woman.

He's twenty-two with lots of experience and he really knows what he's doing. Most of my friends told me the first times are usually painful or not pleasurable but that has *not* been the case. I guess every virgin should get a man of experience." That witch looked at me innocently as if though we were talking about the weather. I was stunned and crushed. I wanted to yell at her, voice my displeasure but I controlled my impulses.

"Is he your man?"

"Of course, he is, or rather he's the only man I'm with. You should know boy that I would never give myself to someone that I didn't consider my man. I'm not like that and you know it."

"Do you love him?" Those words hurt, coming out of my mouth, they tasted vile.

"I love being with him and I love how he treats me and makes me feel but I wouldn't say I'm in love with him. I appreciate and enjoy him. I like him which is more important. He told me he loves me though, but I'm not sure whether he does or not, or if men feel the need to say that to women that they are having great sex with."

"Oh, he's in love with you Cinnamon. Be assured of that." Her wide eyes met mine. I know my voice was showing my anger.

"You sound angry? Why would you be angry?"

"Cinnamon, I'm a bit shocked. I came home to date you. I had no idea you would be... involved." A derisive snort escaped her.

"That's too funny. You treated me like fragile glass since I've known you. Not once did you indicate interest. Last summer you didn't come home or reach out. Negro please." She said before getting up and walking inside, letting the door slam.

Before he could leave her mom walked out. Leigh Dubois was a parole officer and local icon. She sat beside me and stared out at the street.

"I heard your exchange. She's a grown ass woman now... but involved with the wrong man. She thinks I don't know but I do, I also know me saying anything will make him more appealing." Malcolm remained quiet wanting and needing her to expound. "Malcolm, I want her to experience life but not with the likes of Jesse Riley." Malcolm's head jerked up in surprise. Jesse was a year older than him and was the local drug kingpin. He was Cinnamon's best friend, Alexandra's older brother. He was once a high school basketball phenomenon but chose street life instead of college and the NBA.

How the hell did that happen? He wondered.

"If you want her you might want to hang around." Leigh said before going inside. He sat in stunned silence before leaving.

Malcolm drove around a bit before going to the auditorium. Jesse was usually there most days since getting out of prison. He was released recently from his second one-year bid.

Malcolm walked into the auditorium to high fives. Malcolm spent most of his childhood there and was respected by the fellas in the neighborhood. He spotted Jesse playing and saw William Brown, Cinnamon's high school boyfriend sitting on the bleachers. Malcolm decided to pick his brain. Brown stood and hit Malcolm's fist with his, a smile on his face.

"What's up man? How long are you home for?" Brown asked amiably.

"All summer. I've got a job lined up on Wall Street in January. I was supposed to do a second internship in Chicago in September, but I might forgo that."

"That's what's up. You've always been about that money. You probably made a million dollars while in college."

"Nah, nothing like that but I'm doing okay. I'll get a place here for the next few months and see where life takes me. Someone might hire me."

"With a hot MBA at twenty-one, I'm sure they will."

"J. P. Morgan offered me a gig but wants me permanently. I'm good though. What's up with you?"

"I'm working this summer at a real estate company. I have a year and a half left to graduate then I'm getting up out of here." Malcolm knew that was the perfect opportunity to ask him about Cinnamon.

"No woman? You and Cinnamon were hot and heavy in high school."

"That's dead in the water. Clearly, I'm not the man for her. I hear she's seeing him." Brown nodded towards the floor where Jesse was taking a jumper.

"Who?"

"Jesse Riley. No one has seen them together but that's the word."

They watched the ballers play for about thirty minutes quietly. Malcolm mused at how much wasted talent was on the floor. Most had been high school and college stars but flamed out due to police records or drugs and alcohol. After the game ended Malcolm got up to leave. He made sure he walked across the court.

"What's up Riley?" Jesse turned to face him, a grin on his face.

"What's up Black Money? It's been a minute." Jesse and Malcolm were the same height, size and with dark complexions. The startling difference was Jesse's steel gray eyes. His sister Alexandra had the same eyes, but she was much lighter in complexion. The men looked like two sides of the same coin.

"I just graduated college; I'm planning to chill a few months before moving to New York in January."

"That's what's up. I'll see you around then." Jesse loped off, Malcolm watching him.

CHAPTER TWO

CINNAMON

I can't believe he showed up thinking I was just waiting for him. He treated me like a child for years. His ass is crazy. Cinnamon thought as she paced around her room. *He never touched me, kissed me or nothing and he had lots of opportunities. Summer before last I practically stayed at his apartment. Bump him.*

What she wasn't admitting was her feelings for Malcolm Black ran deep but she grew tired of waiting. She dated a few guys including Brown but had been waiting for Malcolm to step up. Last summer and Christmas he didn't bother coming to Center City and she decided to move on. Jesse had been a crush for years and he liked her but respected her age.

I'm going dancing with Alexandra.

Mr. Magic by Grover Washington was playing when Cinnamon and Alexandra walked into Club Owl. The nine minutes long song was one of Cinnamon's favorites. She rushed to the floor and started dancing. She loved dancing and was dressed for it in a chocolate colored sizzler skirt and converse sneakers. The sizzler was a swirling mini dress with matching tap panties beneath. Her long legs were on full display. Geno Hart her favorite dancing partner strutted out to dance with her. Alexandra looked on grinning. She felt a hand on her shoulder and turned to face who dared touch her. She burst into giggles when she saw Malcolm.

"Hey boy, where the hell you been?" Malcolm winked at her and hugged her.

"I'm here now."

"Look at our girl." Cinnamon's hair was flying as she danced with Geno. "She graduated from high school and is a sophomore at the local college already." Malcolm barely heard her; his eyes were laser focused on Cinnamon. The music changed to *Let's Straighten it Out* by Lattimore. Geno pulled Cinnamon closer. Malcolm was stunned she was slow dancing with him.

"Is that her man?" Malcolm asked, keeping his voice neutral.

"No, she doesn't have a man. She's having experiences. I think there is someone but she's not talking about it." It seemed Cinnamon hadn't told Alexandra, or it seemed anyone about Jesse. That was interesting because she and Alexandra shared everything. Jesse was her secret lover.

Experiences huh, I'm here to nip all that in the bud. Malcolm thought. Jesse chose that moment to walk in. He hugged his sister and nodded at Malcolm before posting up on the wall. When Cinnamon finally walked off the floor, she walked past Jesse not greeting or acknowledging him. Malcolm watched his eyes follow her.

"Fancy seeing you again Mr. Black." Cinnamon said sarcastically before scooping her hair off her neck. The gesture kicked into his gut and groin. She was wet from dancing and smelled of soap and perfume.

"Get used to it Ms. Dubois, I might be around until January." He said his eyes meeting hers. "In fact, Ms. Leigh invited me to dinner soon." She rolled her eyes and dropped her hair.

"There you are days late... but I'm sure your dollars are long." She said sarcastically They stared at each other until Malcolm looked away. He saw Jesse watching them, but he didn't move from his post. Malcolm was glad, he wanted a confrontation.

"Come on girl, let's go." Alexandra said.

"We just got here; I'm staying." Cinnamon made her way back to the dance floor, dancing for several songs. Some alone, others with whomever asked. After about an hour Malcolm rolled out.

~~YYYYY~~

"Are you coming to the loft?" Jesse asked Cinnamon when she walked outside close to midnight. She felt peeved and couldn't explain why.

"Not tonight, I'm going home." She said.

"Why, what's different tonight?"

"What's different is I'm going home." She said, walking away.

Alexandra walked outside and Jesse backed away. He watched them get in Cinnamon's Mustang and peel away. He and Cinnamon had been intimate for three months. Like Malcolm he noticed her when she was younger but wanted no trouble from her people, her mom specifically. He was a criminal and Ms. Leigh in law enforcement. But one night he approached her after a night at this club and the rest was history. He was stunned she was a virgin. They were not in a relationship, but they were only with each other. He had fallen in love... he was unsure how she felt but knew they had no future. His mind filled with memories;

She was in the middle of the floor dancing with someone he couldn't remember. Her hair was wet from dancing and her silky psychedelic colored sizzler clung to her. It stopped right under her butt. Her long and shapely legs were on full display. Walking in, he saw her immediately and stood in the shadows watching her. She was all grown up and didn't have a clue how beautiful or innocently sexy she was. He was almost twenty-three to her almost nineteen and she was going home with him that night. He had been out a few weeks and it had been over four years since he touched a woman. He rented a loft downtown over a jewelry store and downtown at night was pretty much deserted. The music slowed down and before she could leave the floor he walked into her space. Squealing she walked into his arms. Let's Straighten it Out by Lattimore was playing, and he wrapped his arms around her, closing his eyes. He loved that she was tall. Her head rested on his chest as he swayed to the music. When the music ended, she could barely breathe. Pulling back, he looked down at her. "Do you have a curfew?" He asked huskily. "No, I'm actually home alone. Mom's away. Of course, the aunts are down the way." She could feel his desire. Neither realized people were dancing around them. "I want you to come home with me... now." Not saying a word, she walked to the bar and reached for her bag, a huge burlap bag with Angela Davis' face on it. He took her hand heading out.

As soon as they were in his loft, he quickly took her clothes off. He was barely able to look at her. Her entire body was the color of golden honey and except for a scar on her side, she was flawless. Dropping to his knees, he placed his tongue on the scar and Cinnamon purred like a cat in heat. That sent desire through him like wildfire and he pushed her to the bed, pulling her legs apart and licking her hard and soft alternately. She exploded, thrashing under his tongue. He wanted to consume her but more than that he wanted to make her his. Standing and ripping off his clothes, he stood before her and her eyes noticed his thickness and desire. He got in bed with her and she took him in her soft hand and he almost lost it. Placing him at her entry, she started rubbing him against her and when he pushed, he met resistance. His eyes opened and he looked at her. "You're a virgin?" He asked in shock.

"Technically but I'm on the pill."

"Are you sure you want to give me this?" In answer she started moving beneath him and as slowly as he could he entered her. "Relax baby... I'm trying not to hurt you."

"Isn't it supposed to hurt a bit?"

Her words sent flames through him and he plunged into her. She wrapped her long legs around him and he was lost to her forever. When she went home two days later, she was Jesse's woman and she was wearing the same outfit she left in.

He shook away the thoughts as he walked to his car. He didn't see Malcolm Black who was across the street eating at the Midnight Cafe.

After showering Cinnamon climbed in bed struggling with her conflicted feelings. Jesse looked different to her after seeing Malcolm. She liked Jesse and enjoyed him in the loft but there was something about the connection she had with Malcolm Black.

CHAPTER THREE

MALCOLM

Malcolm laid low a couple of weeks. He told Ms. Leigh he was coming to dinner on Sunday. He knew Cinnamon would be there for Sunday dinner. Her family was big on traditions. He was in his own place and was mostly reading, working out and planned to take on a few clients for J. P. Morgan. He spoke to the manager who was glad to offer him work. They *needed* black brokers and Malcolm Black came highly recommended.

He saw Jesse a few times at the auditorium and played ball with him, but they hadn't had any conversations. Frankly, he had nothing to say to the man, he planned to take his woman.

For a Saturday afternoon the auditorium was full of ballers from high school age to middle age. Jesse was holding court and Brown was playing.

Malcolm was surprised to see Alexandra and Cinnamon in the stands. He strode over and spoke to them, squeezing in between them. Alexandra scooted over but Cinnamon didn't budge, allowing her shoulder to touch his arm. She felt electrified but refused to budge. Malcolm felt her... fully.

"I'm sorry." Malcolm said turning to face Cinnamon. He was so close he could have kissed her face.

"For?"

"The way I came at you the other day, for not being the friend I am over the past year... I have no excuse other than trying to get it all done. Am I forgiven?" He asked softly. His closeness and handsome face made her dizzy. She rolled her eyes at him trying to control a smile.

"I guess but don't let it happen again. I missed you, you were my boy and you dropped me cold. Your mama told me to drop you cold."

"My mama is mean. Please don't ever do that." Alexandra was listening intently though they were speaking softly, intimately.

"I'll try but you will have to come correct this summer if you don't decide to run off."

"I'm all yours." He said. She grinned and nudged him, hard on his arm with her shoulder.

"Okay... but that involves movies, expensive meals and hardcover books." Something bloomed inside him at her words. She was giving him access to her.

"I'm with it. Are you working this summer?"

"Only four hours a day at the library. I'm working Monday through Friday from nine to one. I also have two classes, otherwise I'm free."

"Cool." He looked away from Cinnamon to the court and saw Jesse looking their way.

At a game interval, Jesse loped over to the bleachers.

"What's up Black, I see you're taking care of my women?" Jesse said, offering his hand. Malcolm took it, shaking it before glancing at Cinnamon. She was looking around the auditorium.

"They're taking care of me. I'm going to dip but Ms. Dubois, I'll see you tomorrow." He stood and Cinnamon stood with him, smiling up at him.

"Okay." Alexandra got up and walked out with Malcolm. Jesse dropped down on the step below Cinnamon.

"What's up with you and Black?" Jesse asked.

"Malcolm has been my boy since I was in ninth grade. He's here for the summer and Mama invited him over for dinner. He's one of her protégés."

He would be. Jesse thought. *College educated nigga with hood smarts.*

"Ms. Dubois doesn't like many."

"She loves a lot of people." Cinnamon said testily. Jesse knew to veer away. He and Cinnamon didn't discuss family, especially her mom.

"Are you rolling through tonight?" It had been three weeks since she came to the loft. For twelve weeks she was there most Saturday nights.

"Not tonight." She said before standing up. "I'll see you soon." Jesse watched her walk to the exits until he could no longer see her. He felt dismissed.

Cinnamon walked out past Malcolm and Alexandra chatting. She waved at them but didn't engage. Malcolm watched her turn onto the interstate which led to her home, not downtown.

"What's up with Cinnamon and your brother?" Malcolm asked. Alexandra looked surprised at the question.

"Nothing I know about. Since he saw her, he's been crushing but he knows better. Ms. Leigh would shoot him in the nuts. You're the one; the two of you have been in love for years."

"How do you figure?" Malcolm wanted to hear Alexandra's take on it.

"Boy please. You were honorable and left her alone and Cinnamon was *never* going to make the first move. Jesse is dreaming."

Jesse isn't dreaming. He's made love to her and is in love with her. Cinnamon on the other hand likes him but isn't in love. It's up to me to insure it doesn't go there.

CHAPTER THREE

CINNAMON

Leigh was whistling in the kitchen and cooking when Cinnamon walked in.

"You're mighty chipper. When did you start inviting young men for meals Mom?"

"Last week. I like young Mr. Black and I recall you were great friends four years ago. Is it a problem?" Leigh asked, peering over the top of her glasses into eyes so much like hers. Cinnamon didn't blink or look away.

"It isn't. I like him too. We just haven't heard from or seen him in over a year, unless you have, and I haven't."

"No, not until he showed up here. He's a good one. I know he has quite a reputation as a lady's man but that's not a bad thing. Women appreciate a man of experience."

"I'm sure that's true. Why aren't women of experience as appreciated? What if I were known as the penis handler?" Leigh's brow lifted. "I mean seriously, he can be known as the G-spot player, but a woman would be a hoe. A part of my charm to men is my untouched quality."

"It's not fair, I admit that. Perhaps it will change in time, but *you* don't need to change it."

"Mom, I'm not that girl, never was. Though I'm kind of with someone sort of, I'm attracted to someone else. I think I'm going to have to break off the current thing."

Leigh smiled inside but nothing showed on her face.

"That's the right thing to do, two lovers at one time is rather messy."

"Quite gross in fact. Do you need me to chop or dice anything?"

"I've got it."

"Okay, I'm going for my run and then I'll shower and change. I want to be presentable for company."

"You do that."

YYYYY

On the way back from her run, Cinnamon saw Jesse parked at the gas station. She was surprised to see him this far out. He lived in town on the west side and they were miles away in what was the countryside. She jogged over to the gas station because her curiosity had the best of her. Her home was about three blocks from the remotely located business.

Jesse got out of his car and saw Cinnamon standing on the other side of his car staring at him. She was covered in sweat and her hair a mass of curly ringlets.

"Hey Jesse, you're off the beaten path." She said lightly but she was suspicious. She knew Jesse knew Malcolm was having dinner with them. He grinned at her lazily, his light eyes piercing hers.

"Unless I'm mistaken, this is free country and even a brother like me can drive around. It's nice up here; it's good to see how the bourgeoisie live and all. There is more black money out here than anywhere in town, it even smells different. My dad used to drive us out here to see y'all Christmas decorations when my brother and I were jitterbugs."

"Ah, slumming backwards, huh?" Jesse's deep laughter filled the air.

"Something like that. I'm always glad to see my baby though. I need... to see you real soon Cin." He said his voice changing but his eyes didn't waver. She didn't look away either.

"We do need to *talk*. Can I stop by the loft tomorrow after work and school?"

"I would like that, say six..."

"Six is good." Cinnamon said, preparing to race the rest of the way home. She felt irked but couldn't say why. Before she could take off Leigh pulled in next to the gas station at the fruit and vegetable stand. She got out and walked over to where Cinnamon stood. Jesse watched her realizing how much like her mother Cinnamon looked. Ms. Dubois was thicker with lighter skin, but they were almost mirror images.

"Hello Mr. Riley." Leigh said.

"Ms. Dubois, it's always a pleasure." Jesse said. Leigh focused on Cinnamon.

"I forgot to get fresh strawberries for the trifle, want to help me pick them out?" Leigh asked.

"Yes ma'am. I hope you made the pudding with real cream and not cool whip."

"Of course, I did. I also made the macaroni and cheese with real cream. Come on." Cinnamon waved at Jesse and followed her mom. Jesse watched them until they were inside before getting in his car and pulling away.

"Jesse is a little out of his way." Leigh said as they filled their basket with fresh fruit. "He passed by the house about twenty minutes ago."

"You could see him from the house?"

"Of course not, I walked out to the road to get the mail from Friday and Saturday. You can't miss that metallic blue color or the sound of the muffler."

"Maybe he wanted to ride through the bucolic neighborhood of the Black bourgeois." Cinnamon said drily, making Leigh chuckle. Her daughter was just like her with that dry wit and smart mouth.

~~YYYYY~~

Malcolm arrived with flowers for Leigh and books for Cinnamon. He embraced Leigh before wrapping his arms around Cinnamon and pulling her close. She was shocked at the sensations that raced through her. She quickly removed herself. Malcolm stared down at her with smiling eyes. He knew she was feeling him, he felt her response and he knew she felt his.

During dinner, they discussed *I Know Why the Caged Bird Sings* by Maya Angelou. Malcolm brought Cinnamon *Gather Together in Her Name* and *Just Give Me a Cool Drink of Water,* both were signed.

"Where did you see Dr. Angelou?" Leigh asked.

"She came to the university. I knew Cinnamon would love them. In addition to being brilliant, she's jazzy, she sang and dance for us."

"That's what happens at Black colleges and universities." Leigh said, glancing at Cinnamon who didn't miss a beat.

"Perhaps I'll go to college in Africa." Leigh snorted and Malcolm chuckled. He loved the way they played off each other. Cinnamon thoroughly respected her mom but held her own with her.

"Malcolm, I don't know what I'm going to do with this grown daughter of mine. I'm going to get bowls of trifle for us and then I'm taking my Sunday afternoon siesta. I need at least three hours on Sunday."

After Leigh was in her room, Cinnamon invited Malcolm to walk with her. They had acres of land and one of her favorite places was a two mile walk to the house her grandmother lived and raised her children in. It was built on 1915 with wraparound porches surrounded by pecan, orange and Japanese plum trees. The house was huge with five bedrooms for the parents and six Dubois sisters. Mr. Dubois and his brothers built it himself. Malcolm followed her intrigued by where she was taking him.

"What's this?" He asked when they reached the secluded house.

"Mom grew up in this house. Grandma lived here until she died ten years ago. I love it here. I think of living here one day." She dropped down on the step and Malcolm sat beside her.

"What were your grandparents like?"

"My granddad-built homes; he built this one and our home. He was a tall, stoic, man with Cherokee blood. He adored grandma who was a dark chocolate spitfire. Grand was tough and loving and the best storyteller. Mom said her mama was Africa and her dad the original American. I spent so much time here with them, the other cousins weren't interested but I loved it." Cinnamon threw her head back with her hands behind her on the porch. Malcolm wanted to lick her neck; instead he traced his finger across it. She glanced at him as his finger lingered on her skin.

"You've zapped me twice today..."

"How?"

"When you hugged me and now caressing my neck. That feels intimate." She said. He swallowed the desire bubbling inside him. He wanted her.

"It is intimate. Cinnamon, I've been feeling you... half in love with you for four years but you were too young then." He paused, watching her.

She said nothing but her eyes were fastened on him. "I came home to date you... but you are otherwise engaged." She closed her eyes, allowing his words to permeate her senses.

"About that other engagement, I need to handle that. I'm feeling you too..."

Delight and desire mixed and mingled inside Malcolm. He leaned over and placed his tongue on her lips. Electric desire sizzled between them. Cinnamon opened her mouth to him, allowing his tongue access. He kissed her with the pent-up love and desire he had been feeling for years. When she moaned into his mouth as she devoured his tongue, he knew he had to stop, or he was going to take her inside. With great strength he pulled away. Her lips were puffy, and she stared at him with undisguised want.

"We need to get back...I have great control but it's about to break." Malcolm said, standing up and placing his hands in his pockets. He was trying to hide his desire but there was no way. Cinnamon finally stood as well, inches from him.

"You're a great kisser. I guess you should go; I'm going to stay out here for a while. Can you find your way back?"

"I can. I want to take you out, are you free Friday night?"

"I am." She stepped closer and kissed him again, lightly. He turned and quickly walked down the path.

She needs to handle her situation. He thought.

I've got to end things with Jesse. Malcolm's kiss is the most real thing I've experienced. He could take me there with just kisses.

Cinnamon returned to the house two hours later to find Leigh on the porch, drinking tea. After Malcolm left Cinnamon went inside the home and sat in her grandmother's chair. That always gave her solace during big decisions.

"Were you at the house?" Leigh asked. They always referred to it as 'the house' though technically it was Cinnamon's house. The grandparents left cash to the four other cousins but the house to someone they knew would love it. The house and ten acres surrounding it.

"I was. I wanted to show it to Malcolm. I've never taken anyone out there since grand died."

"Hmm." Leigh said, smiling as she sipped her tea.

Cinnamon went inside wondering if it were too late to go to Columbia University. She applied and was accepted there, in addition to Howard University in DC, Spelman College in Atlanta and UCLA in Los Angeles. She had chosen locally. She would see where the summer took her, but she was going to mail in her acceptance.

CHAPTER FOUR

CINNAMON AND JESSE

Jesse's gut told him Cinnamon wasn't there for their usual conversation and love making. There was something buttoned up about her including the way she was dressed. Normally she arrived in sundresses with bare sandals and a huge bag. Her attire was the antithesis of that, she was wearing a short-sleeved dress and moderate heels, her work attire and her purse was small. He embraced her, looking down into her eyes.

"It's safe to assume you aren't staying... since its Monday and all." He knew the day didn't matter.

"I'm not. I'm here to discuss us... you and me. Jesse, I need a break from us." He stepped back a bit, his face closing. His heart ached because he always knew this was coming just not yet.

"Define break and what brought this on?"

"A break means we will no longer be intimately involved. It's brought on by me and my own evolution." Jesse smiled but his steel gray eyes were cold.

"So, the break means breakup though other than sex and talk in this room we have never been together. We don't go to movies or dinner. Who do I have to thank for this, Ms. Dubious or the return of the Black Mack?"

"You can thank me Jesse or blame me if that's your preference. I gave myself to you because I really like you. You will always be my first lover..."

"But not your first love because Malcolm Black has that on lock, doesn't he? He's certainly more suitable for you. I guess he can thank me for introducing you to sex." He wanted to bite those words back. Cinnamon's face flushed deeply, and her nose flared. He knew that was uncalled for.

"Don't be nasty Jesse. That's not even necessary. As to the dating thing, you never asked me out.

You brought me here night one and I showed up here ever after. If you showed up where I was you never asked me to dance or engage me, you just posted up and waited. It suited *us.* "

"What would have been the point Cinnamon? Your mom would never approve of me. My sister doesn't even know we are... were together. *She* told me you and Malcolm have been in love for years, you just didn't know it. Look, just go, it's a clean break, no harm, no foul." He said, backing away from her. She saw the food on the table and felt bad, but she knew after kissing Malcolm, there was no going back.

"Jesse, I'm sorry."

"Just go Cinnamon; it's been a sexy three months."

Once Cinnamon was on the stairs, she heard what sounded like dishes breaking. She hurried down the stairwell to her car.

Jesse looked at the broken plates he threw after Cinnamon walked out.

Once Cinnamon was in her car, tears poured. She felt badly about hurting Jesse, but it was better than walking away and saying nothing. She had great times in that loft. The sex and conversation was fun and him giving her books by Iceberg Slim and Man-child in The Promised Land by Claude McKay. She gave him books by Gwendolyn Brooks and Zora Neale Hurston, but she wasn't in love with Jesse, just how he made her feel. She needed to talk to someone. She knew just the person. Aunt Gladys was the perfect confidante.

~~ҰҰҰҰҰ~~

Gladys Dubois was older than Leigh by several years but very close to her and especially close to her niece. Gladys had no children but adored

Cinnamon. She was surprised to see her on a Monday evening but delighted. Her older sister Sara was out of town. Cinnamon wrapped her in a tight hug.

"That's nice baby. Did you eat?"

"No ma'am."

"Then kick off your shoes, I've got baked hen with sausage and sage dressing from yesterday."

"Sounds great."

Cinnamon allowed her aunt to serve her before she started talking.

"Auntie I took a lover three months ago. He's good at sex, better than good but I'm not in love with him. I enjoy him though. The thing is another man who I might really love is back and I don't want... well I broke up with my first lover. I think he loves me though. I hurt him." Gladys reached for her hand.

"Baby, you're just getting started. Good sex shouldn't keep you with a man. Leigh will probably kill me for this, but good sex is just that.

And... It ain't qualified to do the work of love. Live baby, live. That man will never forget you, but men always go on."

"Thanks Auntie."

Cinnamon focused on eating the delicious food. She decided she would stay overnight with her aunt, she always had clothing there. She phoned Leigh to tell her where she was.

~~YYYYY~~

Cinnamon was at the library two hours when Jesse strode in. She looked up from waiting on customers, surprised to see him. He nodded before walking inside, she knew she would find him near crime non-fiction and the motorcycle magazines; those were his favorite things to read. Two hours later, after her shift she found him sitting near the window.

"What's up?" She asked, taking a seat across from him. His eyes lazily roamed over her, in her black mini dress and glowing skin.

"I needed to see you. Cinnamon... I love you; I'm in love with you." He said. His words resonated because she knew that was hard to say.

"Jesse..."

"I know you don't love me and you're so young. I also know your mom would never approve of me, but I thought we had more time..."

"I was taking all of this day by day. Jesse, I've enjoyed every moment with you but sometimes things change quickly." Her eyes pled with him to understand and not make it any more difficult.

"Does that change have anything to do with Malcolm Black returning?" Cinnamon swallowed the lump in her throat. "We aren't that much different, but your mom approves of him."

You guys are worlds apart. Cinnamon thought. *More importantly I love him...more.*

"It doesn't directly have anything to do with him, this is more about me and how I changed quickly." Jesse sat up straighter, leaning towards her.

"Cin, you can't convince me of that. Four weeks ago, you were all in and with me but the minute he arrived was your *change*. You're in love with him but you weren't sure of his feelings. Now that you are, I'm history." The way he said it was painful to hear but as close to the truth as possible. Her heart raced when she first saw Malcolm and she was giddy to learn he was staying awhile. Once he hugged her... her feelings were confirmed and sharing herself with Jesse was no longer possible.

"Jesse, I do have feelings for Malcolm that I need to explore. I'm not going to explore that while with you. I'm not that person. You know that."

"I do but it doesn't feel any better. I also understand, he's hood but educated and Ms. Dubois approves of him. He can take you out, show you off and everyone will applaud that. He probably doesn't even have a parking ticket and I sell smack with a sheet on me." Cinnamon's face flushed. They never discussed Jesse's proclivities. "He grew up three blocks from me, but we were miles apart. I would love that nigga too." Cinnamon watched him stand, her eyes filled with tears. "I'll be around." He said before slowly loping from the library. Cinnamon sat still allowing herself to feel the break.

"Did he do something to you?" Mrs. Rivers, the librarian asked Cinnamon.

"No ma'am, I'm the villain in this story." That's exactly how she felt like a villain. She had no way of knowing how she would have felt months later if Malcolm hadn't returned... but he had. It reminded her of The Spinners song, It Takes A Fool to Learn... that love don't love nobody.

~~YYYYY~~

Jesse drove to his mom's house. Ella Riley wasn't known for her compassion or mothering skills. In fact, Jesse and his brother had been raised by his dad and his wife, but he needed her raw energy and honesty.

He was thrilled to smell fried pork when he walked in, Ella was an amazing cook and cooked all through the day as the mood hit her.

"What brings your ass by?" She asked, pulling a crisp pork chop from the bubbling grease and placing it on a napkin with several others to drain. Ella saw a tall red skinned woman with light eyes, huge breasts and belly but otherwise a skinny woman.

"Can't I visit my Ella?" She snorted but placed two chops on a plate with four slices of bread.

"Sit your ass down and talk then but I know it's about that girl." Ella knew Cinnamon well. Cinnamon loved Ella, talking to her and hanging out at her house. Ella also loved and respected her. They both loved Little Anthony and The Imperials.

It drove Alexandra nuts because she and Ella were toxic at best, but her and Cinnamon vibed. Jesse ate an entire chop before responding.

"What girl?"

"You know damn well what girl. Ever since she's been coming here with Xan, you have been drooling over her. I know you done been with her, I saw it on both of y'all a couple months back. She's cooler with her feelings than you but yo ass..." Jesse chuckled at her words. She saw everything.

"Do you think Xan saw it?"

"Nah, she ain't watching you, she's watching *her*. She wants what you got. It's over ain't it?"

"Something like that. It wasn't meant to last."

"That's for damn sure. You're a criminal and she's a Princess. I can see your appeal to her, but you weren't her boyfriend. Now that Black fella, he's her type. He's got street smarts, book smarts and he's sexy as sin and hell."

Ella's words pierced his gut but he needed it raw and uncut.

"How do you know Black?"

"I know his people. Your sister mentioned he was back and that he's been in love with Cinnamon. She thinks Cinnamon is in love with him too. They match and that uppity ass Leigh Dubois would probably approve. He's a whole package. Hmph."

CHAPTER FIVE

MALCOLM AND CINNAMON

Malcolm arrived on time to pick up Cinnamon and grinned at her black dress, jewelry and sneakers. She knew he always dressed in black. That day it was slacks and a dress shirt with black boots. Leigh looked on with approval.

"Where are you taking her?" Leigh asked.

"The Holiday Inn." Cinnamon quipped before Malcolm could answer. Leigh rolled her eyes, but Malcolm looked stunned.

"Ma'am, we're going to the 1926 Steakhouse for dinner." Malcolm answered.

"That's nice; my sassy mouthed daughter only deserves the Krystal."

"I'll go to the Krystal, sho will and get three burgers and a chocolate shake." Cinnamon said.

"Malcolm, good luck with that one." Leigh said, watching them walk out.

"Why do you tease your mom?" Malcolm asked once they were in his car, his eyes fastened on her.

"Leigh Dubois has to be handled. Otherwise she would run my life. This is a very nice car. Though Cadillacs are for old people."

"I'm older than you."

"Truth, but you and my mom has the same car."

"You're mean Cinnamon, truly mean." She giggled at his description. Mean seemed to attract some men.

~~YYYYY~~

"This feels odd." Cinnamon said after their orders were taken.

"How?"

"You and me on a date. We've had meals in restaurants a time or two, but this feels different. That's it; it feels different, not odd."

"It is different. I want to spend as much time with you as I can. I'm hardcore dating you."

"Okay... where do you live?"

"I found a place on the outskirts. I actually purchased it because I think renting is throwing away money."

"Even if you don't have much money?"

"Especially then. I say get an old house and make it nice. My folks didn't have any money when they got married but they bought a two-bedroom shack. Over the years they added to it and modernized it. Too many think if it's not big and grand..." Cinnamon agreed with him but wanted to hear him explain it. How he thought fascinated her.

"I agree. My granddad always said better a shanty you own than a palace you rent."

"Exactly."

"Can we go see your place?" Malcolm was startled by the question. "What, we used to spend lots of time a couple years ago at your place?"

"Yea but that was then but sure, only if you promise to not try to seduce me."

"Forget it then." Cinnamon said. The waiter arrived with their food, giving Malcolm time to gulp down his water to cool off.

During dinner they discussed school and work.

After dinner they drove around their small but vibrant downtown, stopping to listen to Friday night jazz on the square. The music was good and the atmosphere nice and pleasant.

"Are you going to purchase me a drink?" Cinnamon asked.

"No, you're not twenty-one." Cinnamon snorted.

"Oh, I see, I can't drink but you can kiss me senseless and I'm guessing eventually do other things, but I can't drink!" She sounded huffy and miffed; so much Malcolm stared at her, slightly shocked. She finally laughed. "I was just messing with you. I'm not a good drinker. Now Alexandra drinks like a fish."

"You had me going. This is nice. Do you come often?" He was close and looking down at her. Neither of them saw Jesse sitting on his car across the path.

"Alexandra and I come through here most Friday nights. Sometimes it's not our crowd. Jazz brings out a nice mix of people but sometimes its country and though I like some country music, it's not my crowd. Other times it's other kinds of music. What I love is walking around and browsing. Usually I haven't eaten a steak, so I nosh on food too." Her eyes were holding his as she spoke. He leaned closer, placing his lips lightly on hers, igniting them both.

"You're so damn beautiful." Malcolm murmured.

"Your lips are so damn nice. Can we go?"

"To see my place?"

"Yes, so you can kiss me more thoroughly." Malcolm was so turned on, it was painful.

"Yes, but I need to sit here for a minute, I need a sip of your Icee." She handed him her drink watching him gulp it.

Malcolm stood and reached for her hand. She placed her hand in his. They slowly walked to his car, quietly.

Jesse who was watching them felt impotent with rage and pain but knew there was nothing to be done. He could see how they looked at each other, more painful, how she looked at him. She was as in love as he was.

~~YYYYY~~

Cinnamon walked from room to room of Malcolm's house. It was an older stone house but very well kept. The living room and kitchen were mostly furnished but two of the bedrooms were empty. She stood in the door of his bedroom but didn't enter. It was filled with a huge bed, a dresser and nightstand. The room was gray and black and smelled of him. There were also lots of books and a stereo.

"Malcolm Black, you are such an adult." She said, turning to face him. He was so close to her.

"I've always been. My dad raised a man and I want to live like one. Come to the living room." She followed him, grateful for the opportunity to breathe. His nearness made her giddy. He sat on his massive sofa and she sat next to him. The energy in the room was sizzling. He reached out, pulling her closer before placing his mouth on hers. They kissed, sitting on the sofa for more than an hour. Their bodies other than lips and tongues were barely touching but they were both weak with desire and sweating. Cinnamon finally pulled away leaning her head back on the sofa.

"Are you okay?" Malcolm asked his voice husky. He wanted to devour her, but he wasn't going to yet. Not that night. He was taking his time.

"I am, I'm soaking wet everywhere though, and can I use your bathroom?"

"Of course. I'm going to get us something to drink, coke for you?"

"Please."

After using the restroom, Cinnamon grabbed one of the washcloths from a basket and wiped her face and neck with cold water before returning to the living room. Malcolm had drinks with ice and a huge bag of chips on the table. Two things he remembered that Cinnamon loved. She kicked off her shoes and sat on the sofa with her feet tucked under her before picking up her glass. Malcolm loved that.

"As badly as I want to make love to you Cinnamon, we aren't tonight. Let's take our time."

"Yes let's. Do you watch television?"

"I watch news and sports, not much else." He picked up the remote from the coffee table and turned on the small television. Sanford and Son was on. "Is this good?"

"It's fine. I use television as background noise though my mom and aunts love it. Any show with Black people is a win." She picked up the bowl of chips and started munching them. Malcolm was content to watch her. They ended up watching the show and enjoying it. Afterward they watched Chico and The Man.

"I bet this isn't your usual date." Cinnamon said.

"I don't date."

"Ever?"

"Nah, not really."

"Interesting. I dated a lot in junior and senior year. It was mostly hanging out, nothing serious. Why did you seem angry when you found out I was with someone?"

"Jealous. I thought you would wait until college to... you were such a proud abstainer."

"I was. It's still only been one person. You've likely been with hundreds."

"Hundreds Cinnamon? Don't believe the hype. I haven't been with anyone this year. I've been sexual with several women but nowhere near what folks think. I've been getting educated and working. I know there's a huge double standard with men and women sexually."

"Okay... are you planning to find my g-spot?" Cinnamon asked, looking at him innocently. He felt as if she struck a match to his libido.

"Cinnamon put on your shoes. We need to get out of this house." He rushed to the bathroom, her laughter trailing behind him.

He returned to find her in the kitchen washing the bowl and glasses, with her shoes on.

"It's only ten thirty, what are we going to do?" Cinnamon asked.

"I love driving, do you like riding?" An image of her riding him flashed in his mind. *Yea, we need to roll out.* He thought.

"I do, where are we going?"

"Let's drive to Daytona Beach. We can walk on the beach. Do you have to be home by a certain time?"

"No sir, I'm grown. The beach sounds great."

They spent three hours at the beach, mostly kissing and conversing. At three am, Malcolm drove Cinnamon home with reluctance.

"Today was great." He said as they stood on her porch.

"It was better than great. I'm at the library tomorrow from one to five. I'm normally off on Saturdays but I'm filling in for someone. Meet me there at five and I'll buy you lunch."

"It's a date." He kissed her lightly before saying, "go inside Cinnamon."

He stood on the porch until she was safely inside. He felt like racing around in circles. Cinnamon stood inside the door hugging herself.

CHAPTER SIX

MALCOLM

After working on a few projects for an accountant, Malcolm decided to stop by the auditorium. It was Saturday and there was likely to be pickup games. He ran eight miles in the early morning but wanted to play.

The auditorium was full when Malcolm arrived. He signed in for the next game before posting up on the wall. He nodded at Brown who was waiting also. Brown made his way over.

"What's up Black, are you enjoying your house?" Brown asked. Malcolm used him as his realtor.

"It's great. I'm trying to decide if I need to get another one to rent out."

"Let me know, the market is great. Are you moving home?"

"I haven't decided. I'll definitely be here the next six months until January. I'm working for Morgan part-time."

"Cool, looks like we're up."

Malcolm and Brown were teamed together, and Jesse and another guy were playing them. Malcolm spoke to them, but Jesse barely acknowledged him. They started off good but once they were winning, Jesse got aggressive, so aggressive he shoved his shoulder into Malcolm stunning him. Immediately Malcolm hit him in the chest, knocking the wind out of him. The gym went completely quiet. For several seconds, Jesse was bent over, his hands on his knees, trying to catch his breath. Malcolm calmly watched him as he stood up.

"Riley, if there is something on your chest you might want to deal with it. You're not street handling me." Malcolm said. "You know I'm not the one, ain't nothing changed."

In middle school Jesse and his brother tried Malcolm, thinking he was soft, and both got handled. After that they were cool, but Malcolm *knew* what the new aggression was about.

"Nigga, what could possibly be on my chest?" Jesse asked.

"To put your hands on me something has to be. We either playing ball or doing the other thing, I'm good either way."

Jesse wanted nothing more than to bash Malcolm's face in, but he knew he wouldn't win in a fair fight. In everything Malcolm Black fought to win. He hadn't forgotten when he and Will tried to take Malcolm's bike in 7th grade, and he kicked both their asses.

"We playing or not?" Brown asked. Malcolm nodded and the game resumed.

After the game, Brown asked, "What the hell was that about?"

"You'll have to ask Riley." Malcolm said.

Jesse felt infuriated as he drove home. He hadn't meant to allow another man to get under his skin like that but seeing the intimacy between Malcolm and Cinnamon last night kept him up. The thought of her with another man was too much and especially Malcolm Black. He was known for his skills with women. Women wanted *everything* he offered; Cinnamon included.

Malcolm went home to change, shower and get his mind right before going to meet Cinnamon. He had wanted to crush Jesse's chest and it wasn't just because he touched him. He never started brawls, but he would end one. His dad had been an aspiring boxer and Malcolm spent hours in the gym training with him. He was also a black belt in karate. The fact he loved to dress and was an avid reader many thought he was soft until they started something. His dad told him, "There are three times to knock a man on his ass, if he disrespects your woman, steals your money or put his hands on you."

Cinnamon was sitting at the gazebo outside when Malcolm pulled up. He checked his watch and saw he wasn't late. As he got out, he saw Jesse walk up to the library and stop. Cinnamon glanced up at him from her book. When Malcolm approached, Cinnamon stood, smiling, allowing him to embrace her.

"Hey Baby, what's up Riley?" Malcolm said. Jesse nodded and walked inside. Malcolm wasn't going to address Jesse with Cinnamon. She hadn't named him, only her mom had and Brown. She had just made it clear who her choice was.

"I got off a little early. Do you mind eating at the diner behind here?"

"That sounds good. Wait here I need to go inside."

Malcolm found Jesse and walked up to him.

"Riley, do we have a problem?" Jesse met his stare.

"Other than her... no we're good. You know about me, now I know about you."

"That's fair. She's with me."

"That's clear." Jesse spat. Malcolm nodded and strode from the library. He half expected questions from Cinnamon, but she said nothing. She linked her arm in his as they walked to the Cuban diner.

"I love watching you eat." Malcolm said, watching Cinnamon dig into her flan after eating salad and a Cuban sandwich.

"I love eating. I run walk to stay in shape but I'm going to eat and enjoy. I know so many women who act like they are shy to eat around men. I'm like they see our big butts, so they know we're eating."

Laughter poured from Malcolm. The woman spoke the truth.

Malcolm tried to pay but Cinnamon wasn't having it.

"I invited you and unless you're busy I want you to walk to the theatre with me. *Black Godfather* came out yesterday."

"I'm all yours. So, you like black crime movies."

"I do, it's 1974 and we finally have Black movies, I'm here for it."

Cinnamon spent most of the movie, sleeping on his shoulder. He nudged her when the credits started.

"Was I drooling and snoring?"

"Yup."

"I was tired. I fell asleep about four and the library called at nine asking me to come in early. I need a nap."

"So, you're going home now?"

"No, I'm going home with you. I can nap in your big old bed...unless you're busy."

"Umm, no, that sounds great. Where is your car?"

"Behind the library. I'll follow you."

When they arrived, Cinnamon grabbed a big bag from her trunk.

"I'm spending the night. You can sleep in one of those other rooms if you want. But since you decided you're my man, I'm marking my territory."

Malcolm swallowed down the desire bubbling he had to be inside her.

She's playing with a grown ass man out here. He grabbed her bag and led her inside. He was surprised when she used the restroom, kicked off her shoes and got under the covers, *in his bed.* He was grateful she was the only person other than him, who had gotten in that bed. Within minutes she was asleep.

Three hours later Cinnamon found Malcolm in the kitchen. She sniffed the air; it was redolent with garlic and tomatoes.

"What smells so good?" She asked. Malcolm glanced up from his preparations to see her in an oversized Miami Dolphins jersey, bare feet and her hair loose. His heart surged in his chest. She looked so natural.

"Crab shala. I know you love it. I had some frozen crab just have to make sauce." He watched her climb up on a stool. "You look good in the Mercury Morris jersey. Where did you get it?"

"In Miami. Mom and I are huge Dolphin fans. He's the only Black player with one worth anything." Cinnamon answered.

"You're all about Black, aren't you?"

"Umm hmm. Especially you." She said, making him grin and wink at her. "I didn't know you cooked."

"All of Amelia Black's kids cook, my dad too. In fact, dad and I cook better than all the women.

"Nice. Grandma and Aunt Gladys taught me; Leigh doesn't want anyone in her kitchen."

"Does she know you're with me?"

"She does. I told her I would be with you if you would have me as a guest. She fell out laughing for some reason."

"Because that 'if you would have me' shit is funny."

"I never outright lie to my mom. In my last relationship I didn't lie, I just didn't tell her or anyone..."

"Because it was so special?" He asked, bracing himself for the answer.

"Because it was so temporary. I knew that going in. I was also conflicted but that's a non-issue. Do you have any coke?" Malcolm pointed towards the refrigerator as he minced garlic and reflected on her words. She was young but knew her own mind.

"Are you here to seduce me Cinnamon Dubois?"

"Not at all. I don't have to seduce anyone, even with my limited experience. I'm here because we are in a growing thing beyond friendship and *I* want to spend time with your ass, here."

"Touché, I love that. I want that too and I want you so damn bad, but I don't want *you* thinking *I'm* still that nigga. Cinnamon I love you."

"That my man, friend and lover to be is why I'm here. Now hurry up, I'm starving."

After dinner they sat together on the sofa and Malcolm dozed off with his head in Cinnamon's lap.

"You smell good..." he murmured more than an hour later.

"I'm a clean chick, I wash my coo often."

"Your coo?"

"Yes, that's what my grandma called it. Leigh hated it and wanted me to say vagina. Grandma won." He turned his head, inhaling her scent deeply before licking her thigh. She gritted her teeth against the intense pleasure. His tongue was slightly rough on her soft skin. She forced her legs not to part. He continued his sensual assault for several minutes, just licking and kissing. She groaned when he stopped.

"I've never performed oral sex but Cinnamon I'm going to devour you. Believe that."

"Never ever?"

"Nah."

"I've not performed either, never considered it but for you, anything." Those words turned him hard as a brick. He sat up and grabbed his bottle of water from the table, gulping it down.

"I'm going on my run; will you be okay?"

"Do your thing. I'm going to watch the news. Do you always run at ten pm?"

"I try to run early morning and I did but I need a couple of miles. I'm locking up and taking the key."

Malcolm ran six miles. He needed the stress relief because he wanted to ravish Cinnamon. She was making it hard by inviting herself to stay. He was trying to be a damn gentleman, but she was killing him. He realized he didn't know how to be a boyfriend. They needed to talk.

Cinnamon was snoring on the sofa when Malcolm returned. He rushed to the spare room to shower before she woke. She was sitting up when he walked out in old sweats and white socks.

"How long have you been back?" She asked.

"About fifteen minutes. We need to talk." She stood and stretched.

"Okay, but I need to wash out my mouth and use the facilities."

"So, what's up?"

"Cinnamon, I'm trying to be a good man here, I want to take you out, treat you well and make you love me. I'm not good at all this. But I'm not going to make it. You're so sexy and having you here with me is... hard."

"Do you want me to go home?"

"Hell no. I want to kiss you senseless and bury myself so deep inside you..."

"Then why don't you..." Her words penetrated his brain causing him to stand and pick her up, taking her to his room. He placed her on the bed and stepped back. She pulled the jersey over her head and stood before him in black lace panties and nothing else. Her breasts were mostly dark, hard nipples. He raced to her and dropped to his knees, kissing her stomach. When he licked her navel, her legs spread. He groaned deep in his throat but stood and undressed before her. Her eyes widened at the size of him and his masculine beauty.

"It's okay baby, I know exactly what to do with it. Lay down."

She lay back on his bed and slid her panties down. Like a whisper he was on her and burying his rough tongue inside her. It was so intense she tried to scoot away but he held her firm, devouring her even as she exploded against his tongue. He couldn't get enough of the taste of her.

"You're killing me..." she whispered hoarsely. Moving up he placed his lips on hers.

"You're killing me; you're so damn sweet... I need to get inside you." She reached down and took his silky hardness in hand. A hiss escaped him as she rubbed him against her wetness.

"Malcolm, get inside me..."

He tried to go gently but was unable to. He plunged deep inside her and lost himself there. It was more than any fantasy he had of her. When she started moving with him, he tried to pace himself but when her muscles clenched him, drawing him deeper as she screamed his name, he exploded inside her, his mouth covering hers.

"Oh Baby..."

"I know..." Cinnamon said. She started clenching her muscles and he hardened again inside her. This time he moved slower and deeper, giving her just enough. Their eyes were locked as he loved her.

There was no other way to describe it. He was *loving* her, and it surpassed great sex and orgasms. She felt connected to him on a soul level.

"I feel connected to you Malcolm from my soul..."

"I feel that. I know you're young, hell I'm young but this is real Cinnamon. Nothing touches this."

"Nothing. I guess I did come to seduce you."

"Wasn't much seducing done. I didn't protect you...I've never done that either."

"I'm on the pill and I've never done that without protection, I trust you. You feel good in me."

"You say the sweetest shit. Your forthright honesty is shocking."

"Oh, I'll try to be more duplicitous. I won't. I'm not a gamer, I'm just who I am, no apologies."

"I love that about you. I know I'm heavy."

"Let's roll over, I'll lay on you." He rolled them over, holding her close against his heart. She dozed but he didn't want to close his eyes. It felt like a dream.

~~YYYYY~~

By Sunday evening when Cinnamon prepared to leave, they had painted their DNA over most of the house. They grew freer and more adventurous in their lovemaking. Cinnamon trusted him and that freed her. He loved her and that freed him. Secrets and fantasies dark and light were shared.

"I don't want to let you go." Malcolm said, holding her in his arms.

"I don't want to go but I must. I have school and work next week and though I'm grown I would have to fight mom and the aunties if I started shacking up."

"They would shoot me. I feel like I need to take you home and face Ms. Leigh."

"Don't force the inevitable. I'm sure the time will come when you guys discuss me... even more thoroughly than you did that day on our porch. I *know* she told you who I was seeing and his unworthiness of her precious Cinnamon. Leigh Dubois knows things, but you know that."

She kissed him before grabbing her bag and heading out. He stood in the door watching her until her car disappeared. He was still convinced he was dreaming.

CHAPTER SEVEN

CINNAMON

Cinnamon was grateful Leigh wasn't home when she arrived. She wasn't ready to deal with her. She wanted to soak in her tub and bask in the experiences of the past two days. She felt loved and made love to but also had residual guilt about Jesse.

After getting dressed Cinnamon headed to the kitchen. She knew Leigh had cooked. She was startled when she saw her mom sitting at the table eating. Leigh glanced at her with a smile.

"Fill a bowl and join me. I made chicken and white bean soup, there is sourdough bread." Cinnamon grabbed a bowl and filled it before sitting across from her mom. She blessed her food and dug in. She hadn't eaten since earlier in the morning.

"He didn't feed you?" Leigh asked. Cinnamon's face flushed but she was prepared.

"He did actually. This morning I ate pancakes, bacon and even an egg but it was hours ago."

"Is he your man now or are you still testing things out?"

"We are seeing each other exclusively if that's what you want to know. I'm no longer involved with Jesse, sexually or otherwise. Mom, I know you knew about Jesse and your feelings about him." It was Leigh's turn to flush. "But I was attracted to him and made a decision to be with him. I have no regrets, but I do have residual guilt. He fell in love with me and as soon as Malcolm returned and revealed his feelings and I admitted mine, I had to hurt him."

"Jesse knows the game Cinnamon. I'm not surprised he fell in love with you, you gave him something you can never give anyone else, but he knew there was a beginning and ending. No one in love is ever ready for the ending if their heart is involved. I hope you're being safe."

"Of course, I am. I'm not ready to be a mommy... not even close." They ate quietly until their bowls were empty.

"Malcolm Black is a good guy... not perfect but good. He will *love* and respect you, so love and respect him. He's not one to trifle with."

"You think I trifled with Jesse?"

"Did you?"

"I most certainly did not. When I was with him, I was with him. The minute my feelings changed I told *him*. Mom, I'm not that person." Leigh smiled at the umbrage in her daughter's voice.

"So, stop being guilty and enjoy your life." Leigh said. She got up, washed her bowl and spoon before kissing her daughter on her forehead. "I know it's early but I'm going to bed, I had to go into the prison today."

"I love you mom."

"You better."

Malcolm showered and drove into the city to see his folks. He hoped his dad cooked barbecue. He was starving.

"Someone looks like new money." Malcolm's dad, Melvin said when his son walked into the kitchen. His mom, Amelia looked up at him from her newspaper. Sunday was the only day neither of the elder Blacks works. Melvin was a laborer and Amelia a LPN.

"No surprise to me. I was out at the warehouse early this morning and saw a Mustang parked in his driveway."

"Amelia, you talk too much." Melvin said. "Son, you look happy and relaxed and that's a good thing. Everything can't be about money and education." Amelia ignored them both, she had spoken her piece.

"Thanks dad. I hope there's some barbecue."

"Sho is. There are ribs, chicken and hot links. Sit down; I'll get you a plate."

"Thanks, I want all that and bread." Amelia folded up her paper and strutted from the room. Malcolm and Sr. exchanged looks. They both knew her contrarian spirit.

"Dad, this looks good. Mom is right, I'm with Cinnamon. That's why I'll be around until January. I want her to love me like I love her."

"I think she does. She used to come by asking Amelia if she heard from you. Treat her right son, she's a prize."

"Oh, I know. She's been accepted at New York University and Columbia in January. She will have her own place but she's coming with me."

"Good, good. There are three things not to do, don't get her pregnant, stop her education or ask her to choose you over her people. All those things could come back to bite you."

"Dad, I don't plan to do any of that... though I would love to fill her full of babies." Melvin chuckled deep in his throat. He and Amelia never had that kind of connection. She got pregnant and they got married but at almost fifty he remembered that feeling with someone else. Malcolm would never know but she was Sara Dubois, Cinnamon's aunt. He still *saw* her occasionally.

"I can dig it. Eat your food."

"Thanks dad. I'm trying not to push or rush anything but it's hard. I want her wherever I am but I'm not trying to block her. *She* suggested coming to New York. I was ready to be on a plane every chance I get but we have months."

Melvin nodded in understanding.

"The thing in your favor is Cinnamon is a young woman who's older than her years and likely to marry younger than many, on purpose. She won't need twenty men in her bed to say she had *experiences*."

Malcolm held his hands in a prayer pose.

¥¥¥¥¥

After cleaning up the kitchen, Cinnamon discovered her monthly cycle started. Since being on the pill it was like clockwork. She washed up, grabbed a book and went to the living area. Within minutes she heard pounding on the door. She rushed to answer it and was stunned to see Jesse on their porch. He had never visited her at home. She walked out and gently closed the door. It was near eight pm and fully dark.

"Jesse, what are you doing here? Is Alexandra and Ms. Ella okay?"

"Yea, they're fine; everyone is fine but me. My baby broke my heart." He said and Cinnamon felt pained.

"Jesse..." he threw up his hands as if in defeat.

"I know... the best man won. I just wanted to see you." His eyes roamed over her in her short nightdress. "You're so fucking beautiful. Is there anything I could have done?" Cinnamon's eyes filled. She knew there wasn't anything, but she didn't know how to say that. She had hurt him enough.

"Don't answer that. I couldn't be him or a man your people approved of." He backed down the steps before turning and walking to his car. Tears poured down Cinnamon's face. She went inside and to her room. Leigh heard them but knew Cinnamon needed to grieve this one alone.

CHAPTER EIGHT

LEIGH

Leigh walked into *Steve's Pool Hall* looking around. It was five pm on Monday and she knew it would be full. The pool hall sold food and beer and was a local hangout for hustlers and businessmen. She knew Jesse was often there. She was dressed in navy blue slacks with a lighter blue shirt. Most interestingly she had her service revolver on her hip in a holster. Most people knew her or of her, in fact Steve Lowry the owner of the establishment had gone to high school with her. He spotted her and made his way to her. He didn't want his patrons nervous.

"Hey beautiful." Steve said. "What brings you by?"

"Hey Steve. I'm here to see Jesse, I've spotted him." Leigh strode around Steve to where Jesse was sitting alone, eating. He glanced up. His expression was stoic.

"Hello Ms. Dubois." Leigh pulled out a chair and sat across from him.

"What made you think you could come to my home?" She asked, her hazel eyes focused on his gray ones.

"Clearly, it was poor judgment. It won't happen again."

"Jesse, you need to back away... I know about you and my daughter's time together. I didn't approve of it, but I said nothing, I allowed her to make her own choices but you showing up where I live and making her cry is a non-starter." She saw something like sorrow in Jesse's eyes, but he quickly veiled it.

"Ms. Dubois, like I said it was a lapse in judgment. It won't happen again but for the record I loved... I love her and not once have I compromised her. She came with me on her own accord and she left the same way. I'm not into forcing women to do anything and her age in consideration, Cinnamon is a woman. I'm sure she doesn't know you're here." Leigh chuckled from deep in her belly.

"I could care less if Cinnamon knows because this visit was initiated by you showing up on *my* property. Cinnamon lives with me. Enjoy your lunch." Leigh stood and walked to the bar, ordering a beer. She laughed and talked with Steve and his patrons for more than an hour. Jesse had lost his appetite.

That damn woman is a gangster. He thought before dumping his food and leaving through the rear entrance. *I need to roll out of Center City.*

~~¥¥¥¥¥~~

Malcolm was meeting Leigh for dinner at The Center City Inn. She phoned early in the day, inviting him. He could remember as a child only white people ate there until those like Leigh

Dubois changed things. He wasn't surprised to see her waiting and dressed for dinner in a dress and heels. He didn't know after leaving *Steve's Pool hall* she changed in her office.

Leigh watched him walk in dressed in black slacks, a smoke gray shirt and shiny black boots.

My daughter has excellent taste in men. This one breaks the damn mold. Leigh thought. She stood when he approached her, giving him a hug.

"I felt called before the queen." Malcolm said.

"It's not that. You and I have enjoyed many conversations and you've eaten at my table."

"True but I know it's different now. Ms. Leigh, I love Cinnamon and I'm not going to propose, ask her to quit school or impregnate her anytime soon. I just want to be with her in any way she allows." Laughter flew from Leigh's throat until tears rolled.

"I guess you peeped my game. Malcolm, I feel you're worthy of my daughter and trust me that's the highest praise from me. I do want her to get her degree and I'm far too young to be a grandma. Enjoy being young together, travel, learn and explore."

Malcolm's heart filled. He knew Leigh liked him, but her words proved it. She trusted him with her most precious daughter.

"I want that too. I talked to my dad last night, his advice was similar."

"What did Mary Amelia say?" Malcolm grinned. Very few people knew his mom was called Mary Amelia until she graduated from high school.

"Not much. I mostly converse with my dad about things of the heart."

"That's nice. Men need men. Let's eat and then I need you to follow me home. I think my baby needs you." They talked about current issues. When they were ready to leave Malcolm asked if they needed to order food for Cinnamon. Before Leigh could answer a waiter arrived with two bags.

~~YYYYY~~

Cinnamon was curled up on the sofa when they arrived. Her hair was askew, and she was in her pajamas. She hadn't gone to school or work. She felt melancholy but was mostly past it.

She wanted to flee when Leigh walked in with Malcolm.

"You look beautiful." He said, staring down at her shiny face.

"Thank you but I'm going to take a quick shower. I hope there's lots of food in those bags, I'm starving." She sprinted upstairs and Leigh led Malcolm to the small room where she and Cinnamon ate their meals. There was a sofa, table with three chairs, a television and lots of books.

"I'm going to shower and rest. Thanks for dining with me sir."

"The pleasure was all mine."

Cinnamon returned wearing sweats with her hair in a bushy ponytail. Malcolm had set up her food on plates and gotten silverware and a coke. He pulled her in his arms kissing her.

"Boy, I'm going to eat your lips. I'm so hungry. Where did you find Leigh?"

"We had dinner and she invited me here. Are you okay?"

"I am... I started my monthly last night and Jesse showed up here." Malcolm kept his expression neutral, but he needed to hear more. "He's never done that before. I made it clear he can't do that, and I can assure you Leigh Dubois already talked to him." Malcolm calmed a bit inside. "Malcolm, I'm telling you because you're my man, not for you to do anything." She prayed over her food and dug in.

"So... good. That formerly segregated eatery has good food. These turkey wings are almost as good as moms. Yum."

He watched her eat, allowing the Jesse thing to dissipate. He wanted to confront him but would let this go but if it happened again.

After her dinner, Cinnamon invited him to walk with her.

"Mom invited you because she probably thought I would be in a mood. She calls it the Cinnamon funk because when I'm thrown off balance, I retreat inside but I'm good. I'm glad though. She likes you... a lot."

"I like her and respect her... but you I love."

"That my man is the best part.

They sat on Cinnamon's porch quietly, shoulder to shoulder until she yawned.

"I'm going home now... sleep well and I'll share our summer plans with you in a day or two, now go inside."

Cinnamon leaned into him, placing her lips on his before getting up and going upstairs. On the way to her room, she knocked on Leigh's door.

"Come in." Cinnamon walked in and sat on the edge of the bed.

"Mom, I appreciate everything you do for me but please stop..."

"I'm done but I will never apologize for looking out for you."

"Did you talk to Jesse?"

"I did but not about you but about coming to *my* home uninvited. You never invited him and as such he can't just show up."

"That's fair but I'll handle things going forward. If ever I'm in something and need big guns... I'll call you or Aunt Gladys."

"You got it. Perhaps I shouldn't have invited Malcolm here either."

"Ha ha. Go to sleep old lady and remember who raised me."

Leigh smiled peacefully as her daughter kissed her forehead.

Malcolm forced himself not to find Jesse. He knew it was important to respect Cinnamon's wishes but if he invaded her space again, they were going to mix it up. Little did he know it would be many years before he or Cinnamon saw Jesse again.

CHAPTER NINE

CINNAMON

Cinnamon could barely understand what Alexandra was saying to her. She was crying and babbling through the phone, but she heard Jesse's name. It had been more than a month since Jesse showed up at her home. She hadn't seen or heard from him.

"Xan slow down, catch your breath."

"Cin... they picked Jesse up in Haiti yesterday. He has been over there a month. They say he had several pounds of heroin." Cinnamon's heart dropped. Jesse was a drug trafficker, but he never discussed that with her. She had spoken to him two months earlier about going to Haiti for missions' work and he told her he would go with her because he had been before.

"Oh no. How is Ms. Ella?"

"Mama is mama. Cinnamon they are talking about life in prison."

"I'm so sorry. I'm coming out there." Cinnamon hung up and turned to see Leigh walking in.

"Mom, Jesse is in jail in Haiti. Did you know?"

"How would I know that? I saw him over a month ago. Who told you?"

"Alexandra just called. She's hysterical. Can you find out something?"

"I can try, let me make some calls." Cinnamon waited for an hour. She wanted to give Alexandra some information. The look on Leigh's face when she walked back in wasn't good.

"It's dire Cinnamon. He was arrested with several pounds of heroin as he was trying to board a ship. There were two young women with him from Center City and they are also detained. He's looking at a very lengthy sentence especially if those girls testify against him. They are Shelia Bakers daughters, ages nineteen and twenty." Cinnamon's face blanched. She knew exactly who they were. The eldest, Shana was once involved with Jesse and was down for anything illegal.

"Mom, is there anything *you* can do?" Leigh heard the pleading in her daughter's voice, but she had no jurisdiction over there and Jesse was guilty.

"Not a thing. I have no jurisdiction over there. You do know that's what he does, right?"

"Yes mom, but I've never been exposed to that part of him."

"That's a good thing. Thank God you weren't with him."

"Mom!"

"Don't mom me Cinnamon Dubois. You were talking about missions over there. You could have easily been there. I'm not saying it would have happened but I'm saying it could have happened."

Cinnamon didn't have a response. She knew it could have but it didn't stop her from being scared for him or concerned about her friend and his mom.

"I'm going to see Alexandra."

Alexandra looked haunted and Ms. Ella had a bottle of beer in her hands when Cinnamon arrived. They were sitting on their front porch, Ella on a metal chair and Alexandra on the steps. Cinnamon sat down beside her friend.

"Be glad you weren't with him." Ella said.

"Mama..." Alexandra said.

"Don't Mama me. A few months ago, she was in Jesse's bed and she could just as easily been with him. No good men been tricking good women for years. Those Baker girls know what's what. He came by here with them the night they left. That's the life his ass chose." Ella said before taking a sip from her bottle. Alexandra stared at Cinnamon with questioning eyes. Cinnamon nodded.

"Yes, Jesse and I had a fling. It's been over a while though and we did discuss Haiti but not about drugs. You know I went to Mexico last summer for missions." Ella snorted and belched.

"Jesse ain't no damn missionary. I ain't spending no more time on this. He is the boss and he's paying the cost." Ella got up and went inside.

"Cin, they let him call mama. He told her there was nothing to be done and he's facing life. I'm glad you weren't there too but I am sad for my brother."

"Me too. They sat side by side until the scent of garlic permeated the air. They knew Ella was cooking their favorite garlic fried chicken. "I'm going to stay the night. I need to call mom and Malcolm."

"Okay... the phone is in Mama's room."

Leigh wasn't thrilled but Malcolm understood after she told him what occurred. He didn't tell her the word was already on the streets. He heard it in the barbershop.

"I'm glad they have you." He said.

"I'm glad I have you Malcolm Black."

"Always baby. I'll see you tomorrow."

Long after Alexandra fell asleep Cinnamon sat up with Ms. Ella listening to the blues. She knew she couldn't admit it, but she was hurting for her son. Jesse was good to his mom and neither judged the other. Cinnamon felt she had escaped a very close call.

~~YYYYY~~

The next morning Malcolm came to pick up Cinnamon. She had driven her car, but he wanted her with him. Before he knocked on the door, Ella snatched it open, her eyes drinking in Malcolm.

"Young man, it's a damn sin how fine you are. Cinnamon you better come get this man before I take him." Cinnamon walked around Ms. Ella, placing her hands possessively on Malcolm.

"Ms. Ella, I'll kick your butt about him."

"Baby, I do understand."

"I have my car." Cinnamon said to Malcolm as Ella looked on.

"I know. I want you with me. Leave your keys in the car, my boy will take it to my house. We are going for a drive first."

"Okay... I need to get my bag."

"You're a good one. You might deserve her." Ella said once Cinnamon walked inside.

"Ma'am, I'm trying."

Ella watched Malcolm walk Cinnamon to his car and tuck her in, as a car with two young men drove up to move her car. Alexandra looked over her mom's shoulder.

"Hot damn, that's a man right there..." Ella said. Alexandra didn't say anything. She felt she lost Jesse and Cinnamon at the same time.

They were heading east on state highway forty. Cinnamon knew he was taking her to get pancakes. She loved pancakes and he took her there when he came home from college.

"Are you okay?" He asked.

"I will be. I felt scared when Alexandra called me and worried about her and Ms. Ella. Ms. Ella's acting cool about it, but she's shook up. I can't help but wonder if I had been there."

Malcolm cringed inside because that was his first thought.

"Did you travel with him?"

"No, never but I went to do missionary work in Mexico last year and told him I was considering going to Haiti this year. I could see him offering to come with me if... well you know."

I'm sure his ass would have.

"Don't do that to yourself. You weren't there and he hasn't ever compromised you, has he?"

"Not to my knowledge. Anyway, as Auntie would say that's shit in a well. By the way I'm going to Kingston in September, we still have space." She said, her eyes meeting his. "It's only a week."

"You want me with you?"

"I want you... wherever I am."

"Get me the paperwork and I'm there."

"Okay... can we turn around and go to your house. I'm tired and want to sleep in your bed. No sex though because I'm still on my cycle but you *can* wrap your arms around me."

"That's a bet. I make great pancakes by the way."

Malcolm fell asleep with Cinnamon realizing he relaxed with her. Normally, he slept between midnight and five am most days and he certainly didn't take two-hour naps. He glanced down at her to find her eyes fastened on him.

"What?"

"Why didn't you tell me your feelings sooner?" She asked her voice filled with emotion.

"Initially you were just too young. Then your mom indicated you weren't ready and finally my mom told me to leave you alone, you were too clean for me. You have no idea how many times I regretted not saying anything. I'm glad I finally came to my senses and you were open to me."

"I'm glad too but..."

"No buts baby, we're here now and I'm holding on like a..."

"Muphucka..."

"Yea, just like that. You ready for those pancakes?"

"I am but I need your shower and one of your jerseys."

"You staying?"

"Try to make me leave."

He watched her get up and sent up a prayer. Timing was everything. He got up to get her a jersey. He found her ensconced in his tub up to her neck in bubbles. His heart pounded in his chest. She handed him the washcloth.

"Wash my back..."

"Your butt too?"

"Umm hmm."

CHAPTER TEN

"Do you still live here?" Leigh asked Cinnamon when she arrived home. After leaving Malcolm's earlier she went to school and work.

"Are you kicking me out?"

"Not at all, I'm just inquiring. You left here two nights ago to see Alexandra and her mother. were upset and I didn't hear from you."

"Malcolm picked me up yesterday and I was there. I'm not moving in with him, but I needed and wanted to be with him. I feel a hundred percent better."

"Better is good but I would *prefer* you didn't move in with any man just yet, not even Malcolm Black."

"Mom, I'm not moving in with him, I'm spending time with him. Mom, I spent weekends with Jesse and you never said a word."

"I didn't know what to say. Saying anything was acknowledging it was true. Cinnamon I hated the idea of you with him. Hated! I'm saying it now because I love Malcolm, but I don't advise you or any woman to live with any man. But I'll keep my damn opinion to myself."

"Mom don't get overwrought, I'm not moving in with Malcolm, I have a big empty house and... I can buy a house myself. You *raised* and poured into me. I'm your daughter. Always." Leigh blinked back tears as she stood to embrace her daughter. Cinnamon wrapped her arms around her mother, tightly.

Cinnamon noticed a printout on her bed and sat down to read it. Leigh often left police briefs and things she thought would be of interest or that Cinnamon needed the read. Her eyes widened when she saw what it was.

Jesse Richards Riley of Center City, Florida pled guilty to drug trafficking in exchange for a sweet and unheard-of deal. He was arrested in Port au

Prince, Haiti with several pounds of uncut heroin. Such a haul can carry up to life sentence, but Riley received twenty years and will be serving out his sentence at Florida Correctional Institute in Miami, Florida, a sweet deal indeed. There were two women arrested with him, but they were freed as part of the agreement.

Riley in many ways is an anomaly. He was a better than average student and standout basketball center in high school, leading his team to repeat championships but that was curtailed when he was arrested the month after high school graduation and served one year in prison. He served another year last year and was released sixth months ago. His sentence carries no chance of parole.

Cinnamon read it twice before crumbling it and tossing it in the wastebasket. Her gut told her Leigh was somehow involved in the 'sweet deal' but she would never discuss it with her. That chapter of her life was over.

The Soul Kitchen was full when Cinnamon arrived. She invited Alexandra to meet her for dinner. Alexandra was at the small, black owned eatery when her friend arrived.

"Hey Xan, sorry I'm running late but mama had me drop off something. How are you?" Alexandra shrugged.

"Okay, mom is in a mood. She's been drunk since Jesse got arrested. Did you hear he took a plea? Everyone said he got a great deal because Haitian prisons are bad."

"I'm sure they are."

"Why didn't you tell me you and Jesse had a thing?" Cinnamon had prepared for that question on her drive over.

"It was our thing Xan. There was always a beginning and end point. We were only together in his loft, no meals out, movies or trips. I valued Jesse but he wasn't my boyfriend. He didn't want to compromise me, and I didn't want to deal with my family on this."

"Of course, I certainly wouldn't have approved but mama said he loved you and she's glad y'all had... whatever."

"I'm glad too but that part of my life is over. I care about him and I'm glad he didn't get life, but Xan I must move on. I have moved on."

"I understand that. You and Black are a good look. You love him as much as he loves you."

"I do love him Xan, at this point it's even more because..."

"He came home at the right time." Alexandra said. "Mama said the sun shines on you."

"He did and I'm grateful. I'm going to Columbia University in January."

"Wow, what does Ms. Leigh have to say?"

"We haven't discussed it yet, but I was accepted and I'm going. Xan, I'm not ready to get married yet but I want to be with him, wherever he is."

"I understand. I'll be in Tallahassee but trains and planes."

"Exactly, now let's eat."

Cinnamon knew it was time to tell Leigh because Alexandra was known to blurt things out no matter how she promised not to say anything.

¥¥¥¥¥

"Columbia is an excellent school." Leigh said. "I mean so is Howard."

"Mom, I'm going to Columbia in New York." Cinnamon said firmly. "And yes, it's because Malcolm will be there. I'll have my own place."

"I guess you told me. It's time you flew the coop, I suppose. As you said, I've done all the raising I can do." Cinnamon flapped her arms as if she were flying. Leigh tried not to smile but couldn't help it. Cinnamon was exactly who she raised her to be, smart, independent and stubborn. It would serve her well.

"Maybe, I'll get me a man to move in here." Leigh said.

"You ought to. You're still a good-looking woman with pretty teeth and a good hank of hair."

"You're incorrigible." Leigh said proudly. Her only child was a grown ass woman. She knew the Jesse situation added to that. It taught her things good and bad that would stay with her. She had also learned earlier than most the difference between a man that's good to you and one that's good for you while being better to you.

CHAPTER ELEVEN

Two months later

Malcolm watched Cinnamon administering vaccinations to infants and children and working with babies. Instead of Jamaica they came to Haiti where the need was greater. In August there was a hurricane and temporary shelters and hospitals needed workers. Malcolm worked as a laborer and Cinnamon worked with the medical teams. He saw her with her braided hair unraveling and her body covered in dust as she worked twelve hours days. Her skin was burnished from the sun and dry after one week, but she was dedicated and focused. The next day they were spending a day in a hotel after eight days in a tent.

For the months since Jesse's arrest they had grown closer, doing things together. He taught her how to buy and sell stocks and she had him volunteering more. They read books together, prepared meals and went on what she called ventures; often exploring other cities, their museums and historical landmarks in between her job and school and his work. If it were left up to him a ring would already be on her finger, but he was patient and knew she was committed to him. In four months, they were moving to New York... together. He saw her turn towards him and grin before going back to her tasks.

"That's your girlfriend?" The doctor leading the effort asked Malcolm. He was impressed by both their work ethics. He saw Malcolm's resume and was impressed he still worked as a laborer.

"She is."

"She's a hardworking beauty. Hold on to her. You both have been wonderful. If you ever need a reference, I would be honored."

"Thank you, I'll be working on Wall Street starting in January. If you need a broker, I'm your guy."

"That's even more impressive. Here is my card, reach out to me once you're there. I can send you some contacts."

"Thank you, I appreciate that. I certainly will reach out."

"What's her plan?"

"She's going to Columbia in January, majoring in math and minoring in English."

"That's awesome. Thanks to both of you. You're the future." Malcolm placed the card in his wallet.

~~YYYYY~~

Cinnamon was immersed in the huge tub including her hair. The simple hotel seemed lavish, Cinnamon scrubbed the tub with alcohol and filled it with hot water, oil and shower gel.

"This is divine..." she said.

"That water is boiling. I don't know how you can stand it."

"I'm tough and I was filthy. I needed to boil that dirt off me. My people would be horrified I'm sitting in a hotel tub, but I had to."

"You used a whole bottle of alcohol to clean it. Dr. Abrams want us to join him for dinner downstairs. Are you up to it?"

"Not really but we can make an appearance. All I want is to get in that bed with you naked and later eat Lambi Guisado." Malcolm told her about their conversation the day before.

"Dinner it is. I don't want my man thinking I'm trying to mess up his money. I'll jump your bone afterwards."

"It's bones..."

"You heard what I said Malcolm Black." He watched her ease back under the water.

Dr. Abrams stood when they walked in. His eyes flickered over Cinnamon. Her hair was up in a twist and she was dressed in a snug black dress with ballet slippers. Her only jewelry was pearls and pearl earrings. Malcolm saw the appreciation in his eyes. Malcolm was in black attire as well. Abrams grabbed Cinnamon's hand in his.

"If he doesn't soon place a ring on your fingers, I know a middle-aged Jewish doctor..." Cinnamon smiled, gently removing her hand from his.

"He will sir, I can assure you."

Malcolm pulled out her chair before sitting next to her.

"He's a smart man. I wanted to thank you for your work. You both jumped in and took over. Missionaries aren't born, they're made. Also, Mr. Black I have a check for you to invest for me, January seems so far away."

The servers arrived with platters of food, including the Lambi Guisado Cinnamon mentioned earlier.

For two hours they discussed philanthropy, news and sports. Cinnamon mostly indulged in the delicious food. She was hungry and wanted nothing more than to eat, make love to Malcolm and fall asleep in his arms. The next day they were flying home.

~~¥¥¥¥¥~~

"Doc tried to smooth over flirting with my woman by asking me to invest." Malcolm said after they made love. Cinnamon's head was resting on his chest.

"That was slick. That man must know if I'm with you and there is *nothing,* he can do for me. It was weird we were the only ones he invited to dinner."

"It wasn't weird to me. His ass wanted to spend more time with you even if he had to indulge me to do it. His eyes stayed on you... yesterday he asked if you were my girlfriend. If I had said no, only you would have been at dinner."

"No, I wouldn't have. I only went because you said he wanted to do business with you. I would have politely declined and ate in this room. No thank you very much. Now you can get it again and again." She sat up and straddled him, rubbing herself against him until he hardened and thrust inside her.

~~YYYYY~~

The sisters sipped aged bourbon after eating one of Leigh's gourmet meals. Gladys usually prepared Sunday meals but Leigh cooked and invited Sara and Gladys over. She wanted to tell them about Cinnamon's choice to attend Columbia.

"Leigh, that's an excellent school and they are providing tuition and books." Sara said. "I know you and Gladys wanted her at Bethune or Florida A&M, but it's her choice. I promise you if Malcolm Black had been my man, I would follow him to Timbuktu. Look at how she's bloomed, purchasing stocks and bonds and they even purchased two fixer uppers. They are world changers sister." Gladys didn't respond but she agreed with Sara though she would miss her niece.

"I know but I bet she will be married in a year. I love Malcolm for her, eventually. I saw her graduating from college and going to Europe for a year, globetrotting. Things we couldn't have dreamed of doing in the 50s." Leigh said. Gladys made an annoyed sound with her teeth.

"That's your dream Leigh, not Cinnamon's. Her dream of globetrotting is what she's doing now and taking care of sick children in third world countries. We all knew Cinnamon is a traditionalist and likely to marry young but that won't stop her because she has the right man. That Jesse would have ruined her life and the Brown boy is too immature, he would have caged her but with Malcolm she will do all kinds of things, go all kinds of places. She will be just fine. She's not you... or us...thank God."

"Damn it Gladys, I know but that's my baby. It's not like I can stop her, I'm not even going to try but I already miss her. She told me I should find me a man while I still got good teeth and a nice hank of hair." Sara and Gladys roared with laughter.

"That's our Spicy. She's right though. "Sara said. You're not even fifty; you got lots of juice left. Find you a big, black man to squeeze it out."

"Yes Lord." Gladys added.

"That's why she's like that, spending time with you heifers." Leigh said.

"You mean *us* heifers. Leigh, you're the main heifer who raised her." Gladys said, reaching for the bottle to refill their glasses. They were staying with Leigh. Their Cinnamon was returning the next day and they wanted to be there to greet her. They were all going to miss her.

CHAPTER TWELVE

January 1975

Leigh, Gladys and Sara stood in Leigh's yard watching Malcolm's new car pull out of the driveway with Cinnamon in the passenger's seat. Tears poured down their cheeks. She was on her way to New York and her new life.

"They are really sad." Malcolm said, glancing at Cinnamon. Her face was stoic, but he knew she was sad also.

"They are. I realized all their energies have been focused on me a long time. They wanted me at Bethune which is only an hour away and its Mama and Aunt Gladys Alma mater. I need to do this Malcolm. I love them and I know they love me, but they all stayed here because of grandma. Mama wanted to go to Howard University and got in, but they convinced her to go to Bethune. She got a job teaching in Atlanta, but they convinced her to teach here. Aunt Gladys nursed here because they wanted it. The other sisters flew the coop and rarely came home. It's time now. I'm glad you came home, otherwise who knows." He understood exactly what she was saying. That often happened to smart, Black girls and women, families kept them as close as they could to watch over them, often clipping their wings.

"I'm nineteen but I'm forty in dog years." Cinnamon said and giggled. Her giggles calmed him inside because he was feeling guilty. They had all been kind, but he felt as if he were kidnapping her.

"Are you happy to be leaving with me?"

"I've never been happier Malcolm Black. I know you aren't thrilled I purchased my own apartment but that's a gift from mama and the aunties. They don't want me shacking up with a twenty-two-year-old man." Malcolm's birthday was a month after they returned from Haiti.

"I know. Do they know I bought an apartment in the building next door?"

"No sir. I did tell them *we* purchased a brownstone in Harlem. Aunt Sara loved that. Malcolm, they will miss me, but I know they're proud of me and they trust you for me."

"That's all I can ask. I'm damn sure as happy as I can be. The past six months have been my best... in human years; I'm past my dog years." He started barking and Cinnamon filled the care with laughter.

"So, my *cat* tamed the dog." Cinnamon said.

"Yea."

"Are we driving straight through or stopping? I hope straight through."

"Then straight through it is. I usually do that, but I didn't know if you could handle fourteen hours of sitting."

"Man please. I'm sturdy. It's nine am, we should be there by midnight if we take two thirty minute breaks. Let's do it. I'll even drive a few hours."

"No ma'am, you're not driving me anywhere, you speed and weave. I'm good."

"Whatever, I bet we could get there in twelve hours if I drove but do your thing."

She was sleeping before they got to the Florida-Georgia border as he knew she would be. He decided they would spend the night in Charlotte, North Carolina, the halfway point. He couldn't stop glancing at her, it was hard to believe she was moving to New York, with him.

¥¥¥¥¥

Seeing Jesse behind glass made Ella pause but she quickly gathered herself and sat at the window. He told her to pick up the phone with a gesture.

"Hey..." Jesse said.

"Hey, how they treating you?"

"It's prison but its minimum security. It's the best of the ones I've been in. Lots of white-collar criminals. This is good time." He said, smiling at her. She had to admit he looked well.

"How did you get here Jesse? You were arrested in Haiti with lots of weight." She whispered.

"I think Ms. Dubois pulled some strings. In fact, I know she did." Ella's eyes widened.

"Why would she do that? She doesn't like you."

"I don't think she feels anything one way or the other for me, but she loves her daughter who cares about me. Ma, she's a parole official and very powerful. I was facing life in Haiti. She talked to someone who talked to someone and here I am. I'm grateful because I'm guilty as hell. Twenty years here is good time. I was headed to prison or hell; anyway, here is good." Ella rapidly wiped the tears threatening to spill.

"If you say so. Cinnamon moved to New York, in fact she left yesterday." The smile disappeared from Jesse's face, but he was alert. "She said she's going to Columbia University but she's with Malcolm Black. They've been traveling all summer and buying houses and shit. She's on her way."

"Good for her, she deserves that and more. How's my sister?"

"She's in Tallahassee in college, she's on her way too. Jesse, I think Alexandra just might be the one of us who makes it. She just needs to admit she's a bull dagger and stop the foolishness."

Jesse had to laugh, Ella cut right to the chase and he fully agreed. Alexandra was fully in the closet and because she could tolerate sex with a man wouldn't change it.

"Ma, she wants to be *normal*."

"And I want to be Elizabeth Taylor but that shit ain't happening. We are who we are. We can pretend all we want but that's it."

That truth raced all through Jesse's blood because his time with Cinnamon was pretending for just that time it was something else but where he was who he was. He knew he would always love her, but her life was where she was.

"That my sweet Ella is the coldest truth. Check this out Ma, no more visits. I did the crime, I need to do this time... alone" Ella watched her most loved child, stand up and walk through the gates without glancing back.

When she got in her car, she saw a thick gold envelope.

Don't open until you get far away from here. J. was written in Jesse's block letters. She drove the four hours home, went inside and showered before getting the envelope. Laughter flew from her throat when she saw five fat bundles of hundred-dollar bills. She knew there was several thousand dollars, more than her husband earned yearly in that envelope. Her Jesse was still looking out for his Ella.

CHAPTER THIRTEEN

Racing around her new apartment, Cinnamon was stunned it was already furnished. Gladys had given her a check to purchase a bed, television and dishes etc. but this house was fully furnished, and it was things she loved in her favorite colors.

"My goodness... I am stunned. They told me when we came to purchase the furniture...wait a minute! Malcolm, you did this didn't you?" She asked, swirling to face him. His face was unreadable, but she knew. She leapt into his arms, wrapping her legs around him.

"Black Man, you are so wonderful. My beautiful Black Man." She said against his lips before kissing him thoroughly. From that day forward Black Man became her name for him. He was her Black Man.

"Let's go check out your new bed." Malcolm said.

"Carry me in there, rip my clothes off me and take what you want Black Man."

Malcolm didn't utter a word, but he was always about giving Cinnamon exactly what she wanted.

~~YYYYY~~

After making love twice, napping and showering they drove the few blocks to Harlem. They were meeting with a tenant who rented one of the brownstones Malcolm purchased. He was having the other one refurbished. It would be done in six months and then he was marrying Cinnamon, not dating or becoming engaged but married.

"Oh... they've done a lot already." Cinnamon said when she got out of the car. They had visited two months earlier and they were a wreck, but they were so cheap to purchase they could get great repairs done quickly for the rental.

"They have. Lots of brothers in Harlem need work and I pay cash and weekly. Our side needs a lot more work, but the rental side is done."

A blue 1973 Buick Regal pulled up to the curb. A heavyset, light skinned man got out and looked around.

"Mr. Frederick Williams? Malcolm asked.

"I am and you are?"

"I'm Malcolm Black, I'll be renting you the house. This is my lady, Cinnamon."

"You're the landlord? You're a kid." The man said.

"Sir I own these properties. You've only dealt with the realtor so far. We will be living on the other side sometime later this year, so there will be lots of work being done."

"You and this child here? She's a beauty but y'all mighty young."

"Sir, will our youth stop you from renting this lovely property?" Cinnamon interjected. "If so, there are other tenants." Malcolm and Frederick looked to Cinnamon. She had the stony Black American Princess look.

"No ma'am, I'm sure you're mature adults. Let's start over... I'm Frederick Williams and I'm here to see my new home. I'm widowed with two grown children and I have three pensions." He offered his hand to Cinnamon who shook it firmly.

"And I'm Cinnamon, too young co-owner of this fine establishment." Malcolm watched the exchange play out. Cinnamon was a lot of women wrapped up in an innocent *looking young* package. She was country born but her city shit was slick.

"Well, it's mighty kind of you to allow me to live in such a fine establishment and to one day be your neighbor. Please show me inside." He offered his elbow and she linked hers in his and threw her nose up while winking at Malcolm.

"Malcolm, we need your services. Chop chop!" She said imperiously. Malcolm raced around her, waving the keys and grinning.

"Yes ma'am Ms. Cinnamon. I am glad to be at your service." Cinnamon ignored him saying to

Mr. Williams, "Good help is so hard to come by but he's a big strong buck, so I'll keep him."

"I'm sure you will, and that man will be glad to be kept. Whipped like cream." Malcolm almost fell, laughing at Williams' quip and Cinnamon with her nose still in the air. He snatched open the door for them and swatted Cinnamon's butt.

"Mr. Williams, he whoops me too." She screeched. This time Mr. Williams laughed harder than Malcolm. During the whole exchange Cinnamon held her nose up with her lips tightened and pinky poking out.

"Lord, you two are complete fools. This is the most I've laughed in years. Ms. Cinnamon you look snooty, but you are funny. Lord." Mr. Williams said after he stopped laughing. Malcolm was still tickled. Cinnamon was a certified nut.

~~YYYY~~

"How did you get in here?" Mr. Williams asked. They invited him to dinner after the inspection and they were at Sylvia's Soul food restaurant. Sylvia's opened in 1962 and in thirteen years had become *the* soul food restaurant in New York, catering to locals, movie folks and national celebrities. It took hours of waiting to get seated.

"I called two weeks ago and made a reservation sir."

"Well, damn, I guess that's all it takes. Your young people are out there, in a good way. It does this man's heart good. Makes me very proud."

"Please don't start crying Mr. Williams... we're trying to eat here." Cinnamon said. "Be the old man you're trying to be."

Williams looked to Malcolm.

"What are you going to do with Ms. Cinnamon here, one minute she's the Black Queen Elizabeth and the next minute Shotgun Sally?"

"Mr. Williams, I done told you he beats me!" Cinnamon said sounding pitiful. Malcolm shrugged and cut into his chicken.

"Both of you are crazy." Mr. Williams said. "This is the best chicken." Malcolm winked at Cinnamon, making her smile back, sexily.

"Cinnamon, you are always making promises." Malcolm said. Cinnamon smooched at him.

"Not here children, not here." Mr. Williams said. Cinnamon and Malcolm filled the air with laughter. Mr. Williams was a keeper.

"I had no idea you were so crazy Cinnamon."

"I'm sure... you were focused on my innocence, while ignoring me, now it's because you're so focused on my other charms. Stick around you'll get to see all of me. And since *we are* going to be moving to Harlem next to Mr. Williams in a few months you might be thinking about changing my name, otherwise I'll be in Manhattan."

That's my Cinnamon. I think she just proposed to my ass. They were quiet several minutes, her mouth was tight, but she spoke first.

"Can we just drive around?" Cinnamon asked. "I mean like Brooklyn or somewhere we haven't seen yet. I want to see it all."

Malcolm felt her eyes on him. He was going to make a point.

"Cinnamon, I would have already married you if it were up to me. Of course, I want to take you to Harlem as Cinnamon Black. The delay is on you."

"I know that. I do need a little more time, but I want to be Mrs. Black, I do."

"Okay, let's ride then."

They drove through several areas and through downtown going down every street before going home to make love and sleep in Cinnamon's bed. They had yet to move into Malcolm's place. It was fully furnished, and the kitchen stocked but there was something they both loved about her smaller apartment. It felt like home.

CHAPTER FOURTEEN

For the next three months Malcolm and Cinnamon were like ships passing in the night. He had a required twelve weeks to trader training working fifteen-hour days. Cinnamon was taking a double class load from eight to three and tutoring from five to eight. When Malcolm arrived home Monday through Friday around ten pm, she was passed out on the bed. In addition to school and tutoring she was the bookkeeper for their growing real estate business. On Saturday they did chores, errands and went out. Sundays were spent in bed with sex, books, newspapers, food and sleep.

"Next week I'm working eight to seven. I'm off the fifteens." Malcolm said at Saturday evening dinner. They had spent most of the morning running errands and wrapping up homework.

"That's great. I think I'm giving up tutoring. I'm exhausted, I just wanted to stay busy while you worked." She said and yawned for affect. Malcolm reached in his pocket, pulling out a folded paper and sliding it across the table. After perusing it she looked up at him, her mouth ajar.

"What is this?"

"That Ms. Dubois is twelve weeks of earning. We could purchase a big ass house or ten more fixer uppers."

"Wow, this is... wow. Do it then Black Man. I'm proud if you." She got up and started doing a little dance. He joined her with his fraternity step.

"Man, that's great." Cinnamon said plopping on the chair.

"It is. And so is this..." he slid a two-carat ring from his pocket and slid it on her finger.

"Cinnamon Dubois, you will be Cinnamon Dubois Black in three months. Period. You and me, we are going places." Cinnamon held up her ring for a few seconds looking at it before side glancing him.

"So, where we going?"

“Anywhere we want to.”

“Well yes then!” He grabbed her and danced her around the restaurant. *Dream Merchant by New Birth* was playing on the jukebox as they danced close together.

EPILOGUE

Current Day

Cinnamon read and reread Malcolm's novella several times, a smile on her face. For two months she saw him working furiously on his laptop. He told her it was his fiction debut.

"So, what do you think Madame?" Malcolm asked. Cinnamon glanced up from the manuscript.

"I have a question. Are you going to leave our real names in this book?"

"I damn sure am. This is how it would have been if I opened my damn mouth that day on the porch. It's the truth even the Jesse parts. I know Ms. Leigh helped him get twenty years because of you so I just fictionalized that a bit. The truth is in what would have happened if... what could have happened and that's what I wrote. It's going to be a bestseller. I might write another novella." Cinnamon rolled her eyes, but she loved it because she would have loved it if that happened with one exception, her kids, but it was great.

"You're really good I must admit. I guess only Jesse could be upset and my kids."

"Jesse has nothing to do with this, I gave him his props in all things. I could have killed his ass off. As for the kids, they are born and living well. They're going to be like Jasmine Sullivan said and pick up their feelings. This is my story."

"They all read this and approved, didn't they?"

"Hell yea. I'm not letting them sue me because I wrote my fantasy. I have ironclad agreements from all of them, except Labyrinth but she knows. They collaborated all the way but if you insist, I can change the names."

"No, let's go bold. Jesse told some of this is his *little* book. So, do your worse. Who's publishing this?"

"*Malcolm Black Books* is publishing. I've been in bed with a famous publisher for years and I've learned all the tricks. I have an attorney in Aura Black, a distributor Thane Whitton and you

Cinnamon Black has already edited it because you can't help it."

"You know you make me sick!" She said.

"That's why I got your medicine." She snorted but was thrilled. She knew it would cause gossip and blind items in newspapers.

"You do and I'm all in on this, but I want a lot more sex. I mean, deep, down dirty, wet sex. We got all this property in New York City; I want us doing it in the elevator on the train and all those homes. Even outside on the stairs in the first brownstone." Malcolm stood and started unbuckling his belt.

"Oh, I have all the filth you can stand. Now get those clothes off and show me what you want in the book."

Cinnamon got up and slowly stripped, grinding sensually at the sexy Black Man who loved her like *that*.

THE FALLOUT: Malcolm's Queen II late April 2021.

The Fallout will continue in current day.